There are a lot of stories about that creepy-looking mansion on the hill, but Danny Crowe's living one far creepier than anything he's heard. His adventurer Grandpa promised him they'd explore the mansion one day, but a freak accident killed his gramps and put that plan in the ground until Madame Leota, a ghost in a crystal ball, reached out to Danny to deliver a message: His Grandpa's ghost is in the mansion, and needs his help!

Danny plucked up every bit of courage he had and set out for the mansion, learning that the house is populated with retired ghosts. Most want to relax and enjoy their (after)lives, but a sinister spirit known only as the Captain has found a way to trap the ghosts inside. Only a living person can free the mansion and Grandpa's spirit, so Danny agreed to help. After being granted the ability to see ghosts, Danny was led to the Grand Hall, where Pickwick was leading a meeting to discuss their predicament. But the Captain's dark magic has clouded the ghosts' minds, turning the meeting into a grand party. Now, even Danny's fallen under the sway of the hall: He has no idea why he came to the mansion, but is determined to never leave the party!

Welcome, foolish mortals, to...

The Haunted Mansion

3

Danny

Madame Leota

The Captain

Pickwick

JOSHUA WILLIAMSON writer   JORGE COELHO artist   JEAN-FRANCOIS BEAULIEU colorist

VC's JOE CARAMAGNA - letterer   E. M. GIST - cover artist

BRIAN CROSBY - variant cover artist   JOHN TYLER CHRISTOPHER - action figure variant cover artist

ANDY DIGENOVA, TOM MORRIS, JOSH SHIPLEY - Walt Disney Imagineers

EMILY SHAW & MARK BASSO - editors   AXEL ALONSO - editor in chief   JOE QUESADA - chief creative officer   DAN BUCKLEY - publisher

special thanks to DAVID GABRIEL, BRIAN CROSBY & CHRIS D'LANDO

ABDO Spotlight   Disney KINGDOMS   MARVEL

ABDOPUBLISHING.COM

Reinforced library bound edition published in 2017 by Spotlight,
a division of ABDO, PO Box 398166, Minneapolis, Minnesota 55439.
Spotlight produces high-quality reinforced library bound editions for
schools and libraries. Published by agreement with Marvel Characters, Inc.

Printed in the United States of America, North Mankato, Minnesota.
092016
012017

THIS BOOK CONTAINS
RECYCLED MATERIALS

marvelkids.com
© 2016 MARVEL

**Elements based on
The Haunted Mansion® attraction
© Disney.**

PUBLISHER'S CATALOGING IN PUBLICATION DATA

Names: Williamson, Joshua, author. | Coelho, Jorge ; Beaulieu, Jean-Francois,
    illustrators.
Title: The haunted mansion / writer: Joshua Williamson ; art: Jorge Coelho,
    Jean-Francois Beaulieu.
Description: Reinforced library bound edition. | Minneapolis, Minnesota : Spotlight,
    2017. | Series: Disney kingdoms : haunted mansion
Summary: When a ghostly woman appears to Danny urging him to come to the
    haunted mansion and help his dead grandpa's spirit, Danny enters the house
    and agrees to help the spirits trapped inside, that is if he can survive.
Identifiers: LCCN 2016949392 | ISBN 9781614795872 (v.1 ; lib. bdg.) | ISBN
    9781614795889 (v.2 ; lib. bdg.) | ISBN 9781614795896 (v.3 ; lib. bdg.) | ISBN
    9781614795902 (v.4 ; lib. bdg.) | ISBN 9781614795919 (v.5 ; lib. bdg.)
Subjects: LCSH: Apparitions--Juvenile fiction. | Haunted houses--Juvenile fiction. |
    Grandfathers--Juvenile fiction. | Survival--Juvenile fiction. | Graphic novels--
    Juvenile fiction.
Classification: DDC 741.5--dc23
LC record available at https://lccn.loc.gov/2016949392

Spotlight

A Division of ABDO
abdopublishing.com

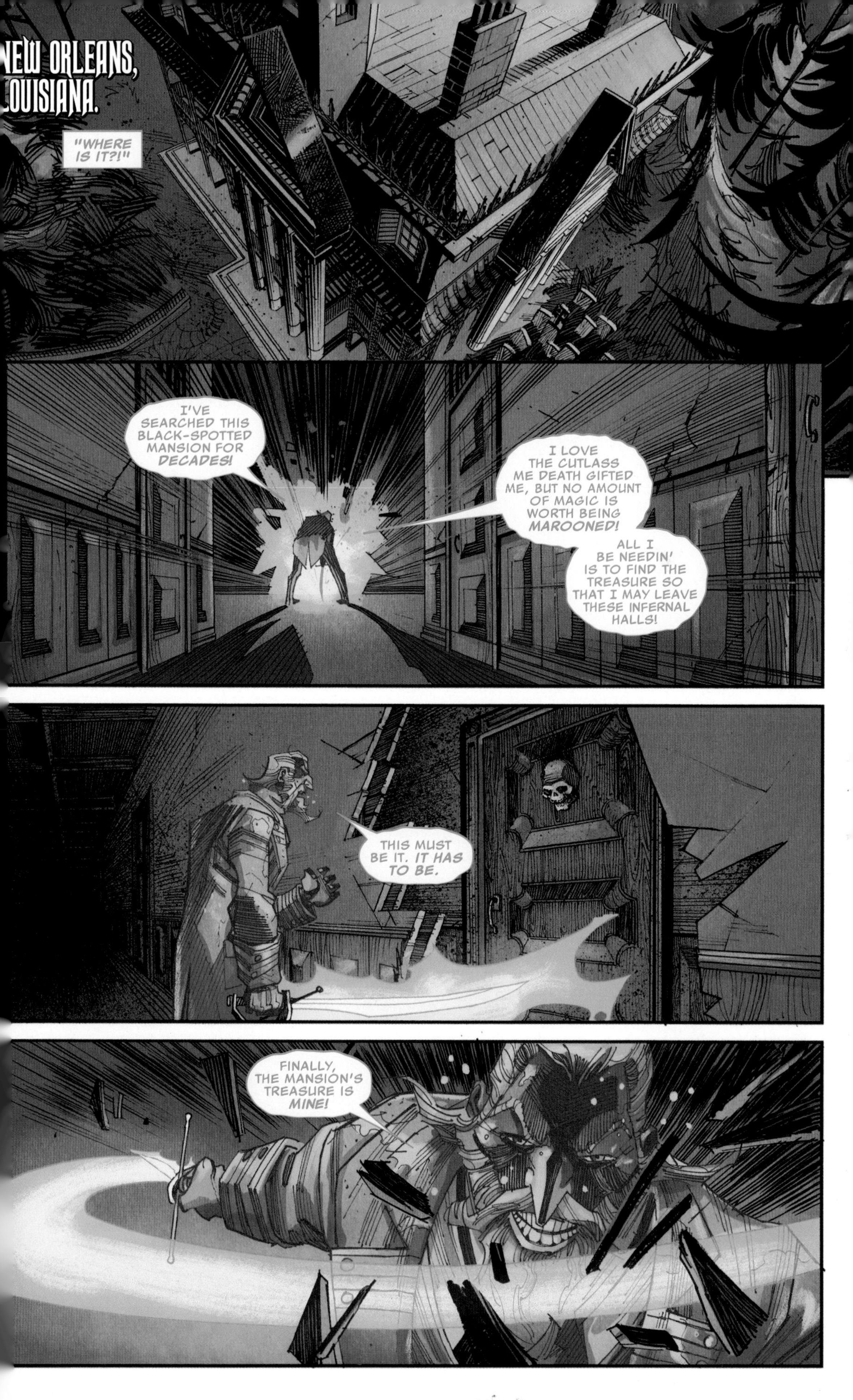

NEW ORLEANS, LOUISIANA.
"WHERE IS IT?!"
I'VE SEARCHED THIS BLACK-SPOTTED MANSION FOR DECADES!
I LOVE THE CUTLASS ME DEATH GIFTED ME, BUT NO AMOUNT OF MAGIC IS WORTH BEING MAROONED!
ALL I BE NEEDIN' IS TO FIND THE TREASURE SO THAT I MAY LEAVE THESE INFERNAL HALLS!
THIS MUST BE IT. IT HAS TO BE.
FINALLY, THE MANSION'S TREASURE IS MINE!

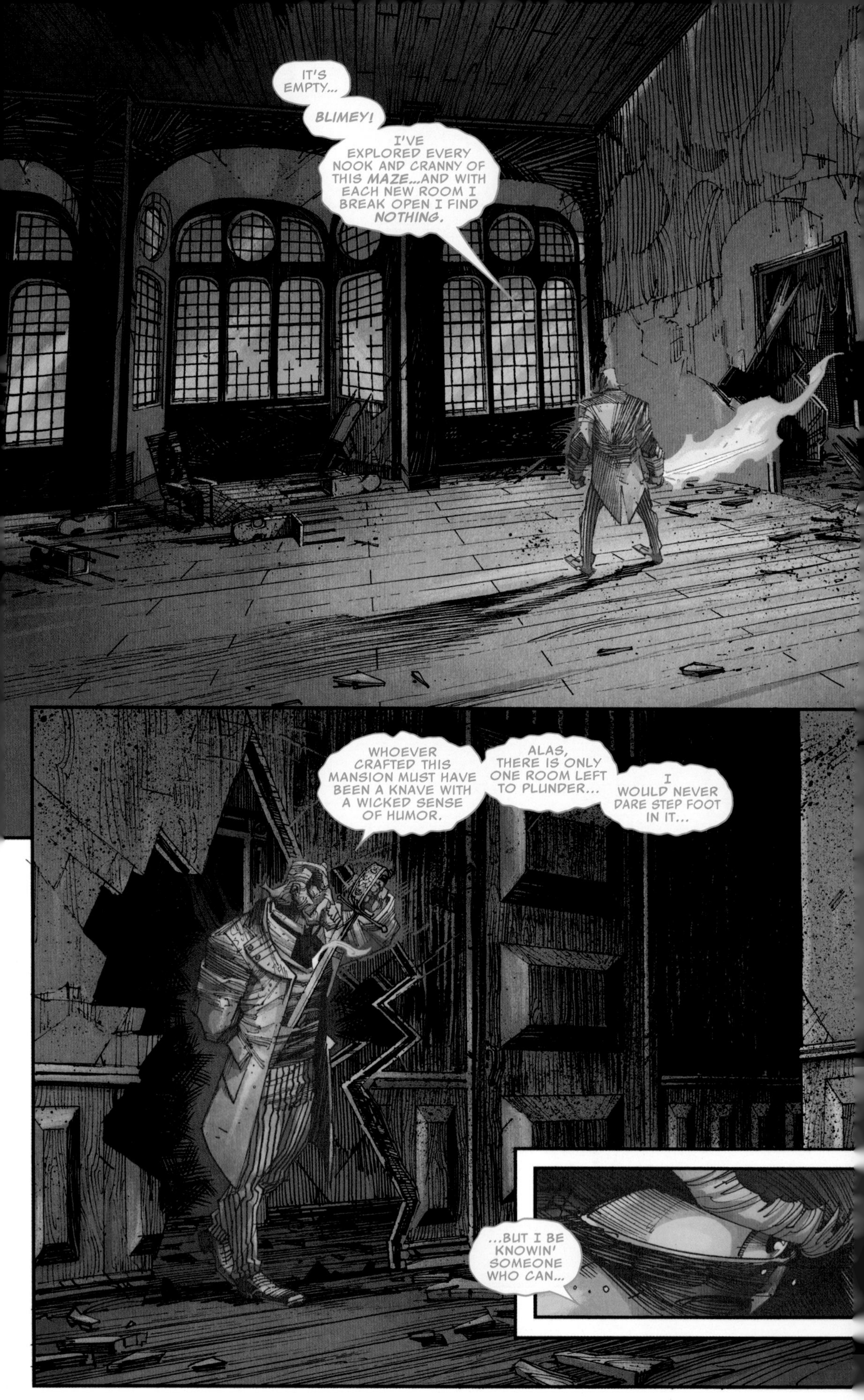
IT'S EMPTY...
BLIMEY!
I'VE EXPLORED EVERY NOOK AND CRANNY OF THIS MAZE...AND WITH EACH NEW ROOM I BREAK OPEN I FIND NOTHING.
WHOEVER CRAFTED THIS MANSION MUST HAVE BEEN A KNAVE WITH A WICKED SENSE OF HUMOR.
ALAS, THERE IS ONLY ONE ROOM LEFT TO PLUNDER...
I WOULD NEVER DARE STEP FOOT IN IT...
...BUT I BE KNOWIN' SOMEONE WHO CAN...

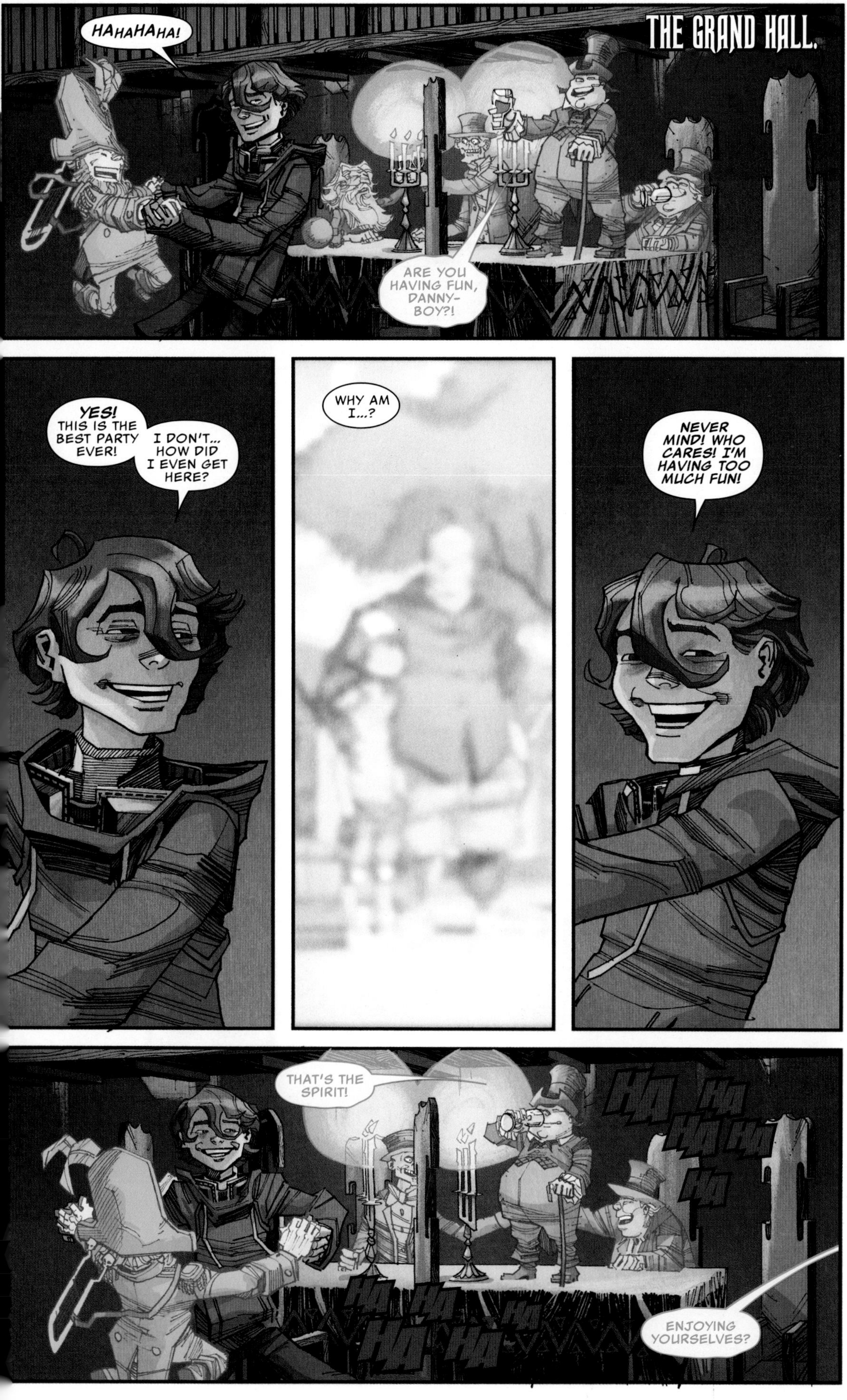
THE GRAND HALL.
HAHAHAHA!
ARE YOU HAVING FUN, DANNY-BOY?!
YES! THIS IS THE BEST PARTY EVER!
I DON'T... HOW DID I EVEN GET HERE?
WHY AM I...?
NEVER MIND! WHO CARES! I'M HAVING TOO MUCH FUN!
THAT'S THE SPIRIT!
HA HA HA HA HA
ENJOYING YOURSELVES?

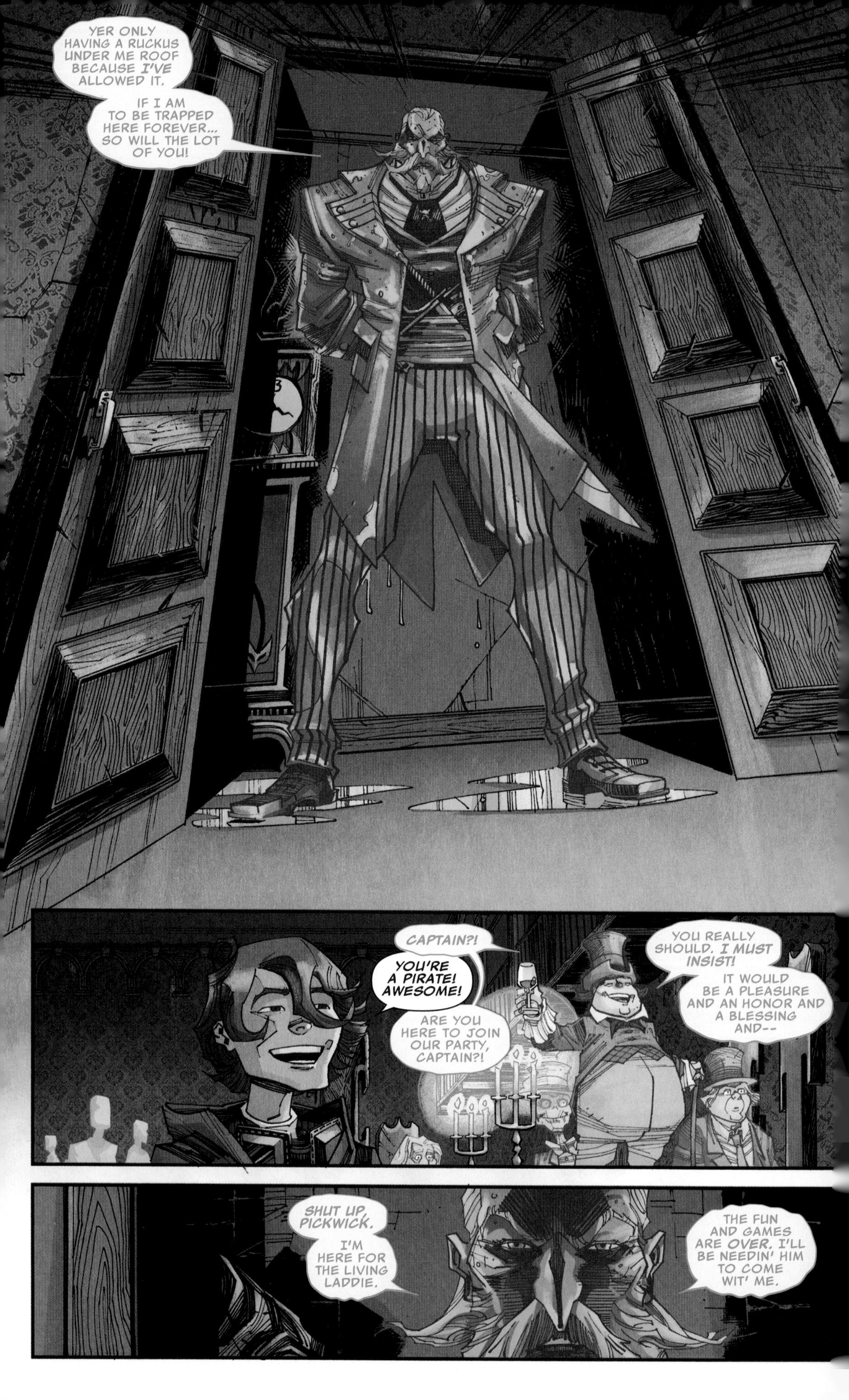
YER ONLY HAVING A RUCKUS UNDER ME ROOF BECAUSE I'VE ALLOWED IT.
IF I AM TO BE TRAPPED HERE FOREVER... SO WILL THE LOT OF YOU!
CAPTAIN?!
YOU'RE A PIRATE! AWESOME!
ARE YOU HERE TO JOIN OUR PARTY, CAPTAIN?!
YOU REALLY SHOULD. I MUST INSIST!
IT WOULD BE A PLEASURE AND AN HONOR AND A BLESSING AND--
SHUT UP, PICKWICK.
I'M HERE FOR THE LIVING LADDIE.
THE FUN AND GAMES ARE OVER. I'LL BE NEEDIN' HIM TO COME WIT' ME.

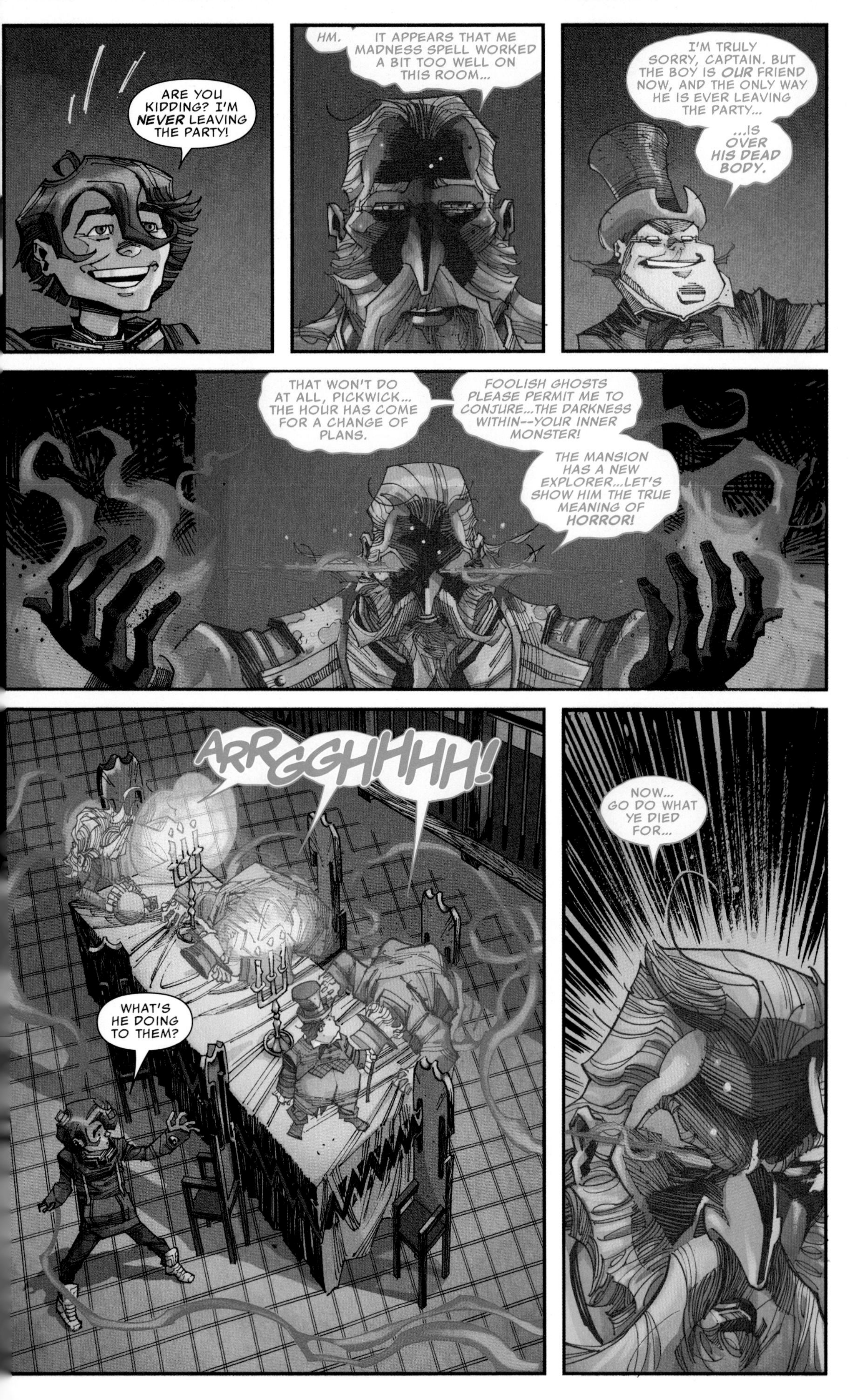
ARE YOU KIDDING? I'M NEVER LEAVING THE PARTY!
HM.
IT APPEARS THAT ME MADNESS SPELL WORKED A BIT TOO WELL ON THIS ROOM...
I'M TRULY SORRY, CAPTAIN. BUT THE BOY IS OUR FRIEND NOW, AND THE ONLY WAY HE IS EVER LEAVING THE PARTY...
...IS OVER HIS DEAD BODY.
THAT WON'T DO AT ALL, PICKWICK... THE HOUR HAS COME FOR A CHANGE OF PLANS.
FOOLISH GHOSTS PLEASE PERMIT ME TO CONJURE...THE DARKNESS WITHIN--YOUR INNER MONSTER!
THE MANSION HAS A NEW EXPLORER...LET'S SHOW HIM THE TRUE MEANING OF HORROR!
ARRGGHHHH!
WHAT'S HE DOING TO THEM?
NOW... GO DO WHAT YE DIED FOR...

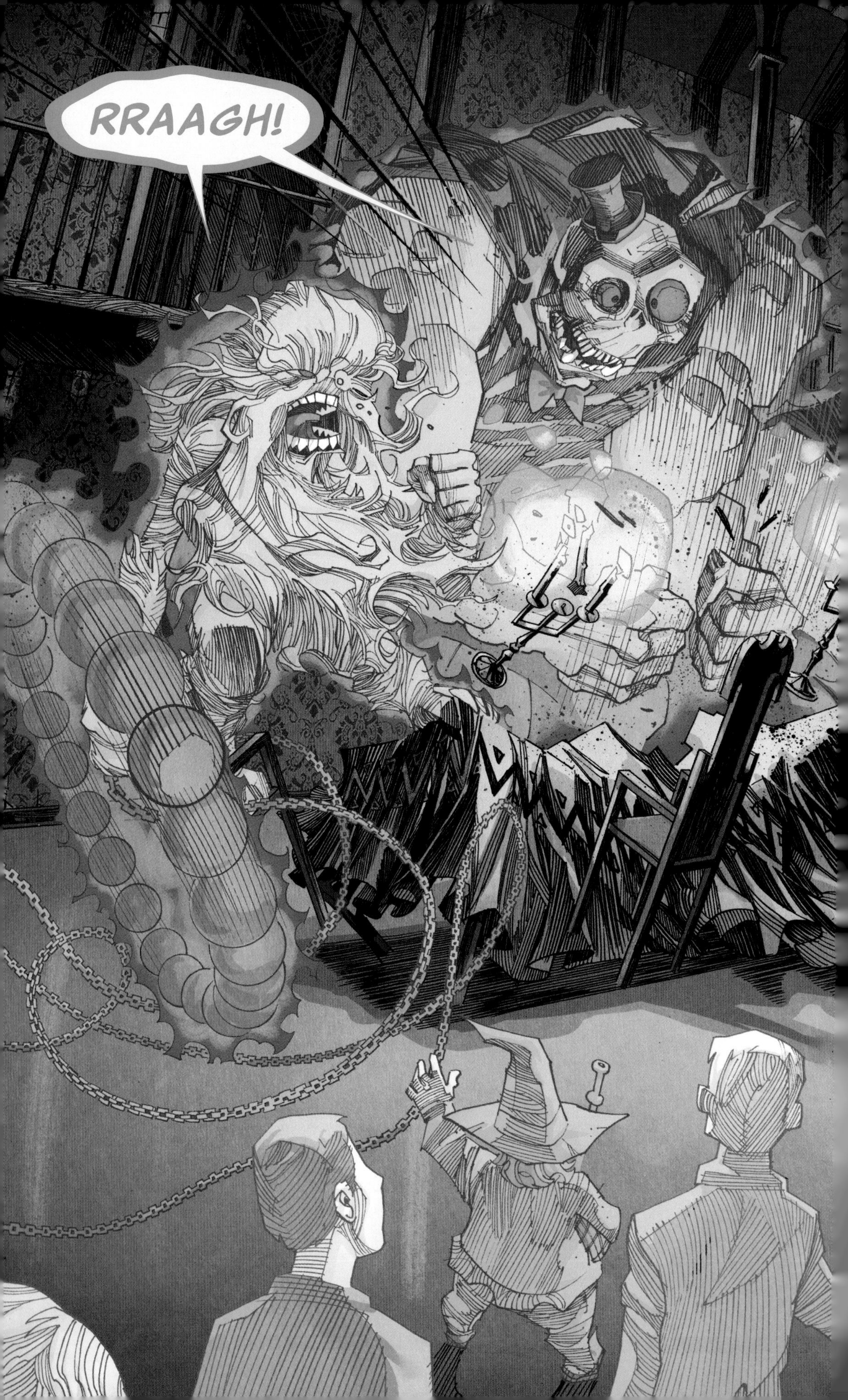
RRAAGH!

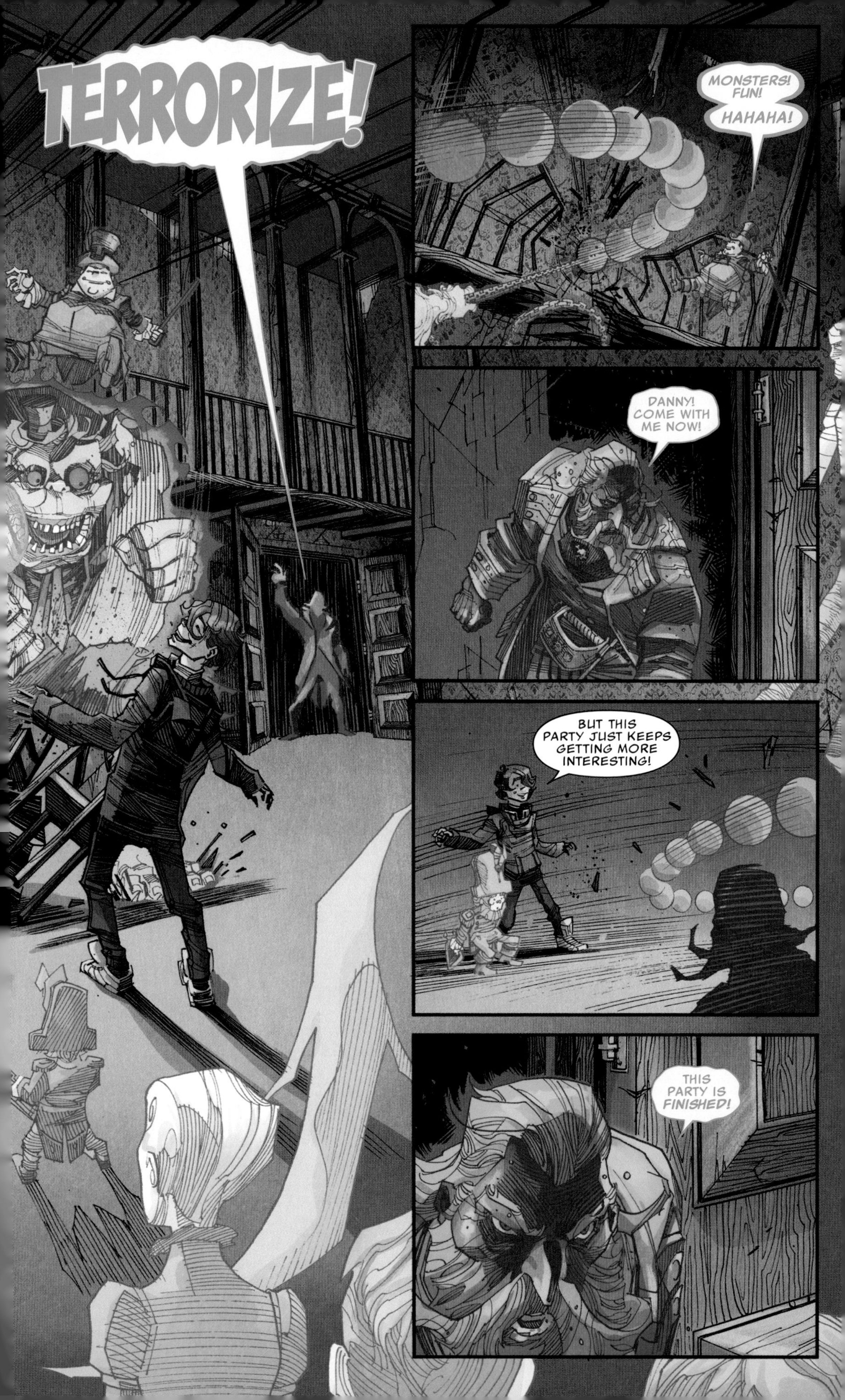
TERRORIZE!
MONSTERS! FUN!
HAHAHA!
DANNY! COME WITH ME NOW!
BUT THIS PARTY JUST KEEPS GETTING MORE INTERESTING!
THIS PARTY IS FINISHED!

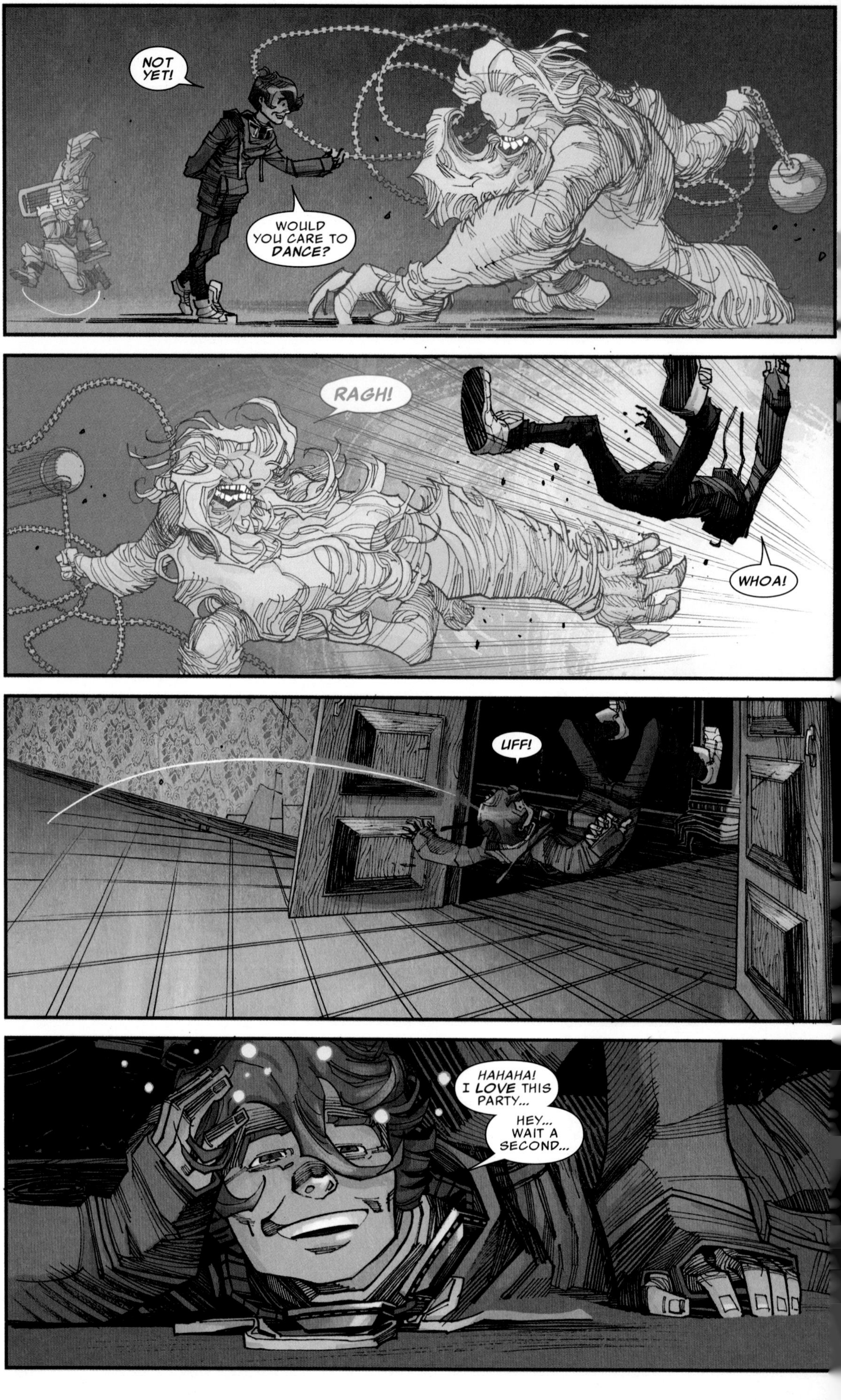
NOT YET!
WOULD YOU CARE TO DANCE?
RAGH!
WHOA!
UFF!
HAHAHA! I LOVE THIS PARTY...
HEY... WAIT A SECOND...

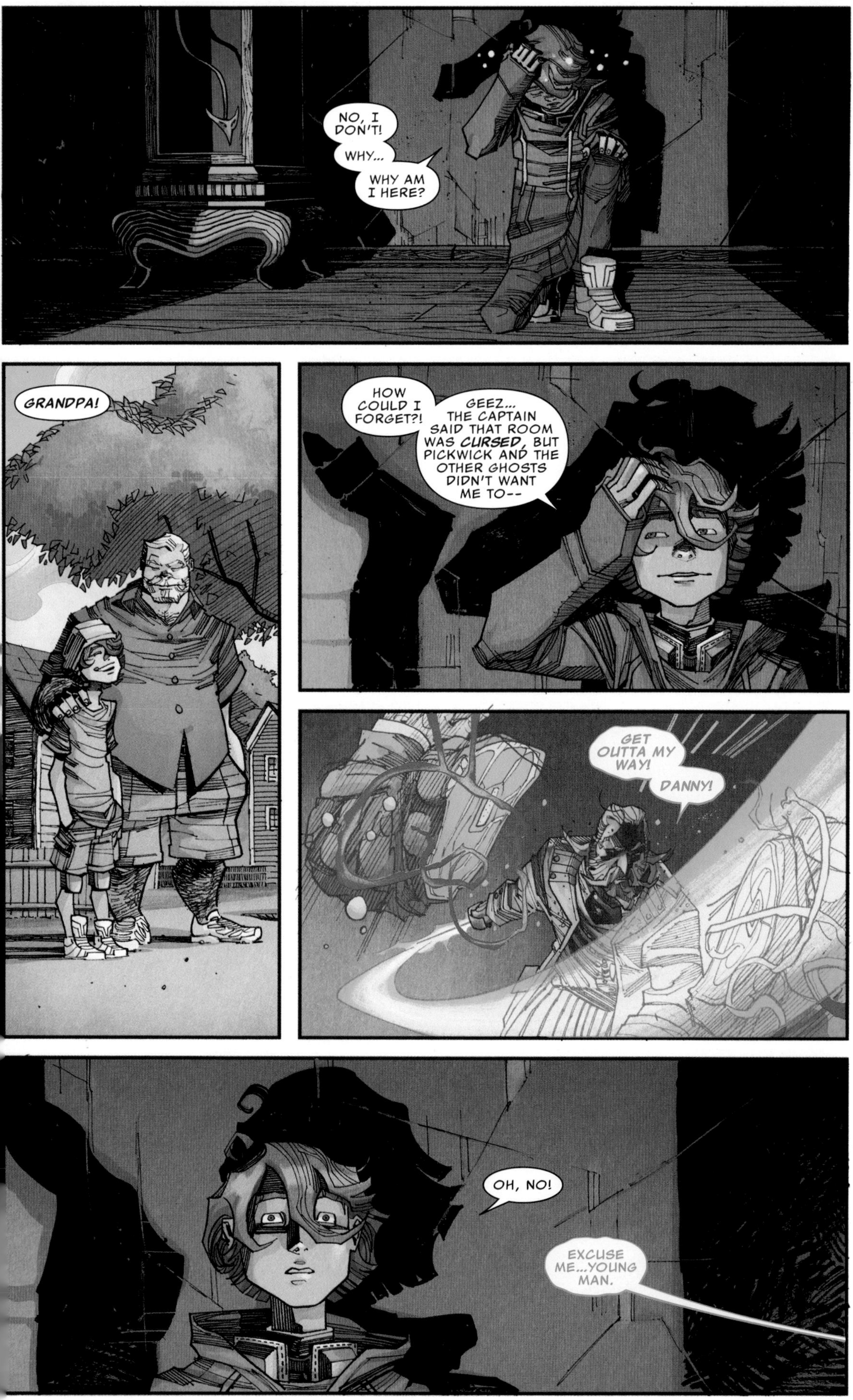
NO, I DON'T!
WHY...
WHY AM I HERE?
GRANDPA!
HOW COULD I FORGET?!
GEEZ... THE CAPTAIN SAID THAT ROOM WAS CURSED, BUT PICKWICK AND THE OTHER GHOSTS DIDN'T WANT ME TO--
GET OUTTA MY WAY!
DANNY!
OH, NO!
EXCUSE ME...YOUNG MAN.

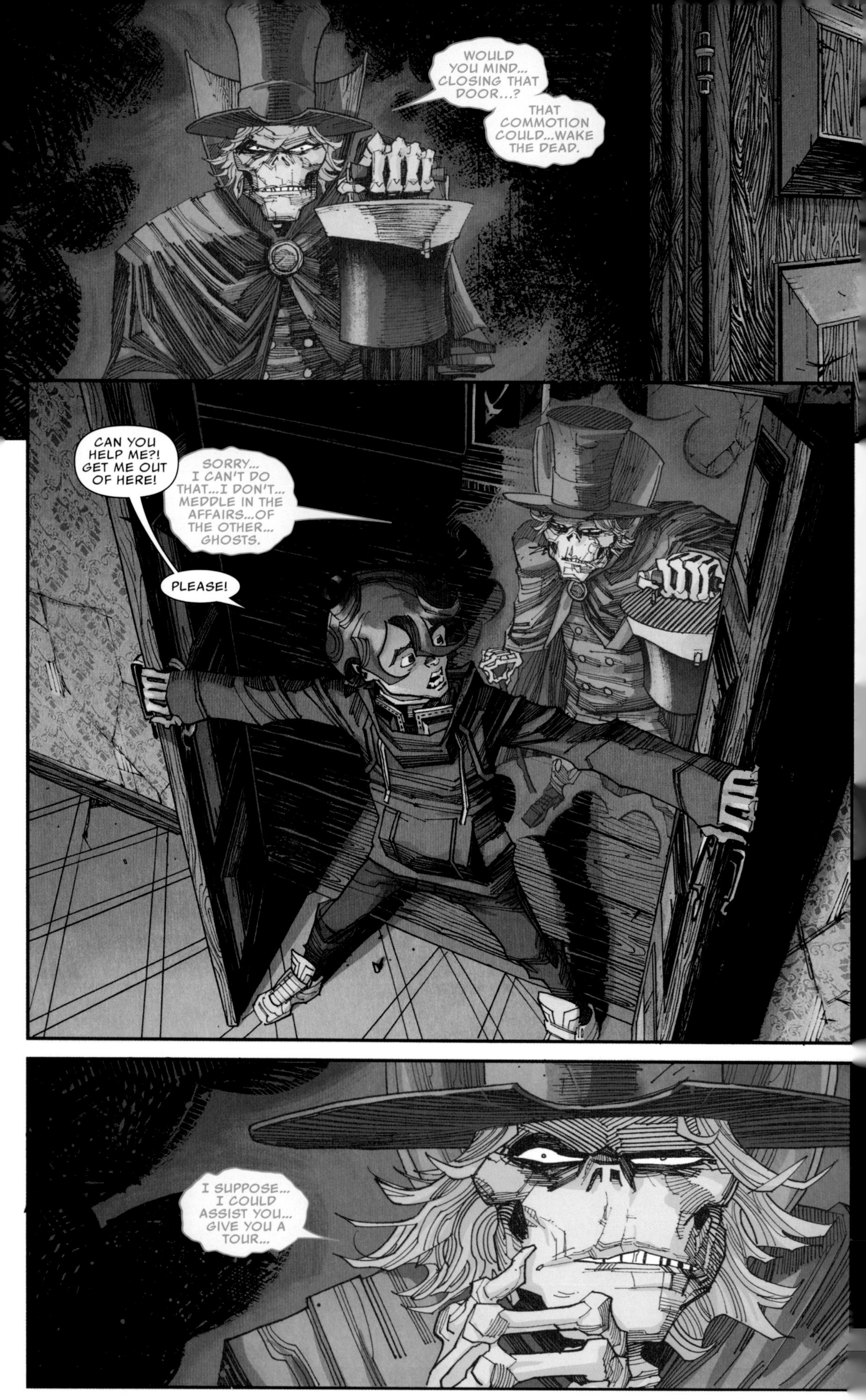
WOULD YOU MIND... CLOSING THAT DOOR...?
THAT COMMOTION COULD...WAKE THE DEAD.
CAN YOU HELP ME?! GET ME OUT OF HERE!
SORRY... I CAN'T DO THAT...I DON'T... MEDDLE IN THE AFFAIRS...OF THE OTHER... GHOSTS.
PLEASE!
I SUPPOSE... I COULD ASSIST YOU... GIVE YOU A TOUR...

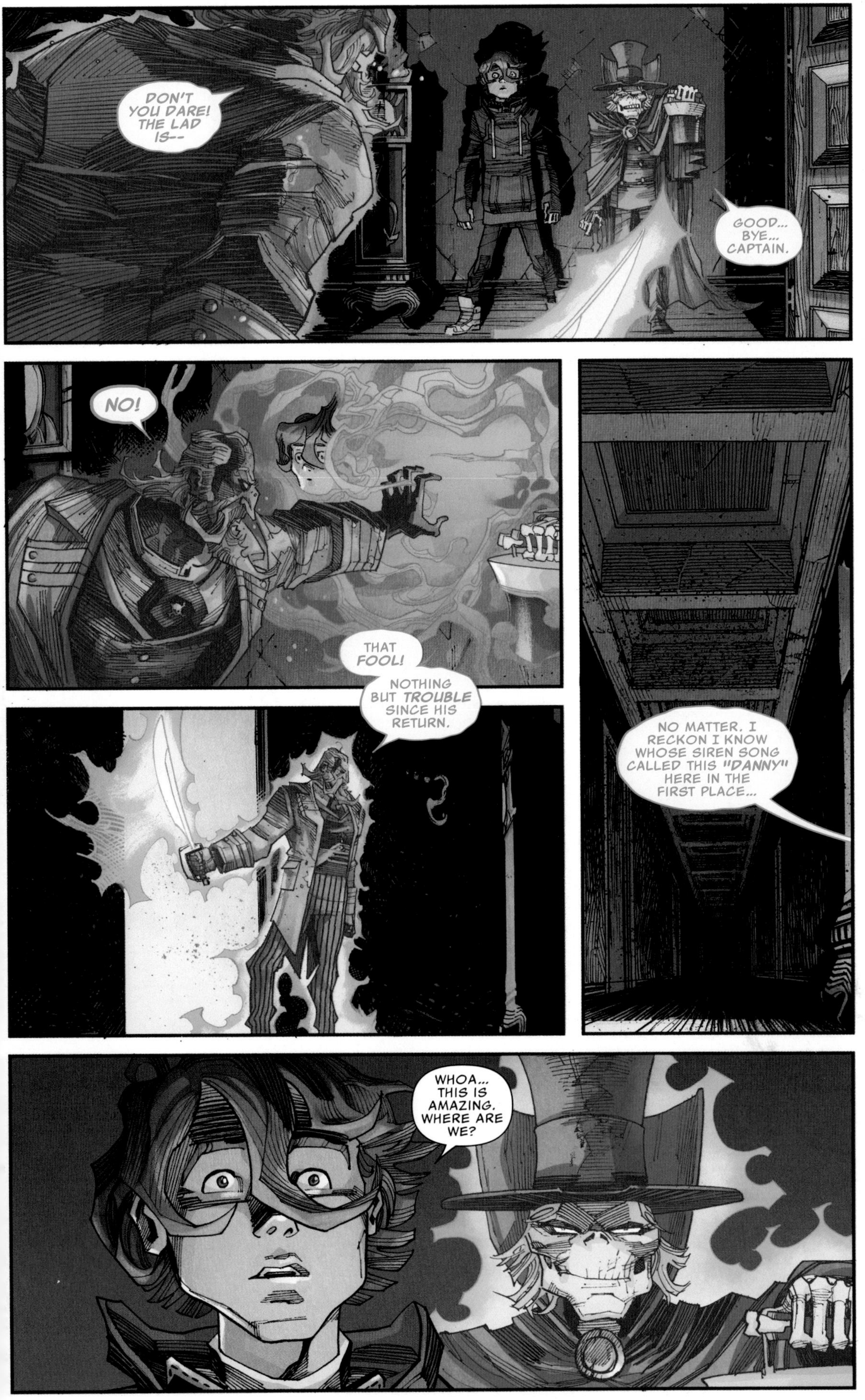
DON'T YOU DARE! THE LAD IS--
GOOD... BYE... CAPTAIN.
NO!
THAT FOOL!
NOTHING BUT TROUBLE SINCE HIS RETURN.
NO MATTER. I RECKON I KNOW WHOSE SIREN SONG CALLED THIS "DANNY" HERE IN THE FIRST PLACE...
WHOA... THIS IS AMAZING. WHERE ARE WE?

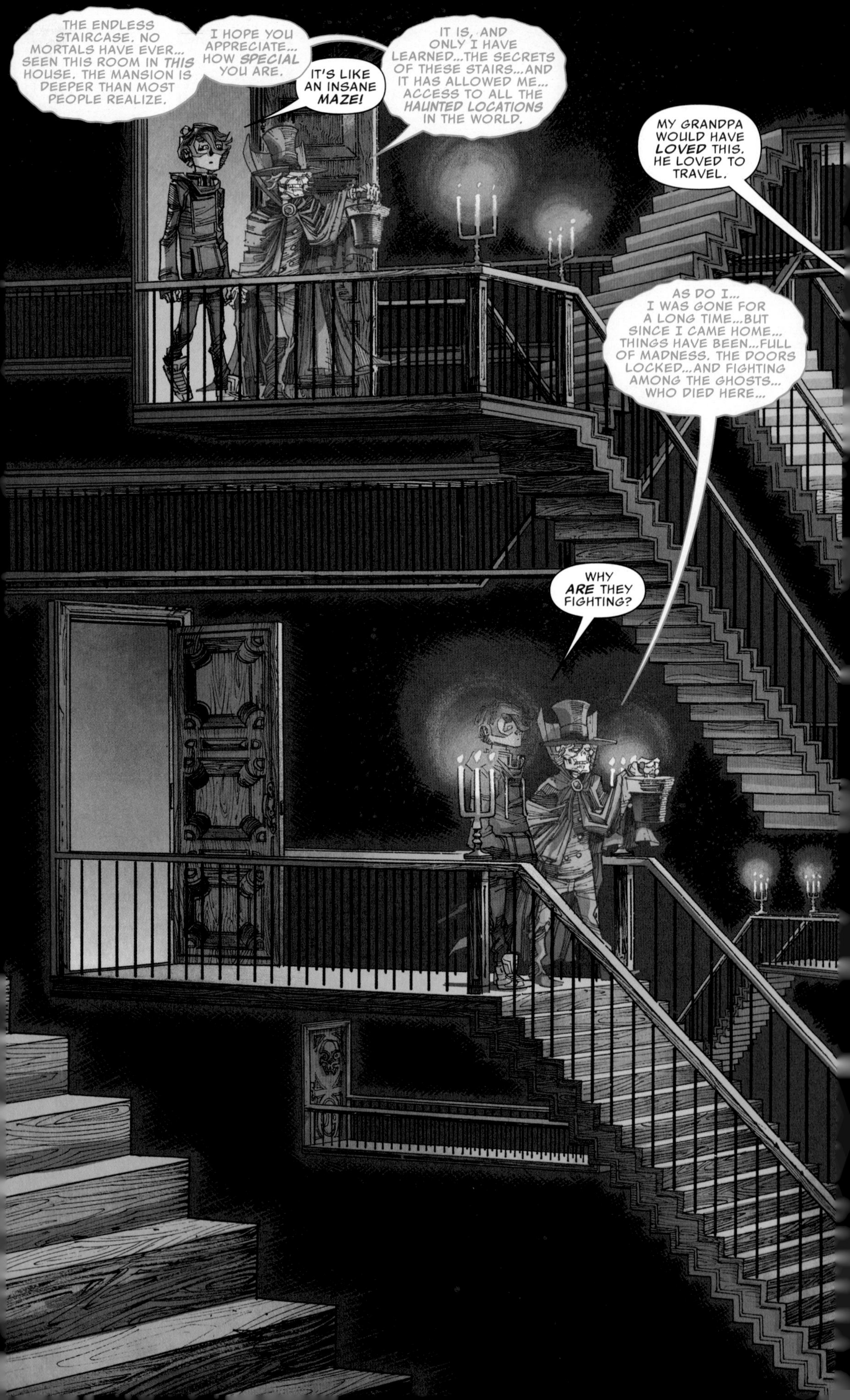
THE ENDLESS STAIRCASE. NO MORTALS HAVE EVER... SEEN THIS ROOM IN *THIS* HOUSE. THE MANSION IS DEEPER THAN MOST PEOPLE REALIZE.
I HOPE YOU APPRECIATE... HOW *SPECIAL* YOU ARE.
IT'S LIKE AN INSANE *MAZE!*
IT IS, AND ONLY I HAVE LEARNED...THE SECRETS OF THESE STAIRS...AND IT HAS ALLOWED ME... ACCESS TO ALL THE *HAUNTED LOCATIONS* IN THE WORLD.
MY GRANDPA WOULD HAVE *LOVED* THIS. HE LOVED TO TRAVEL.
AS DO I... I WAS GONE FOR A LONG TIME...BUT SINCE I CAME HOME... THINGS HAVE BEEN...FULL OF MADNESS. THE DOORS LOCKED...AND FIGHTING AMONG THE GHOSTS... WHO DIED HERE...
WHY *ARE* THEY FIGHTING?

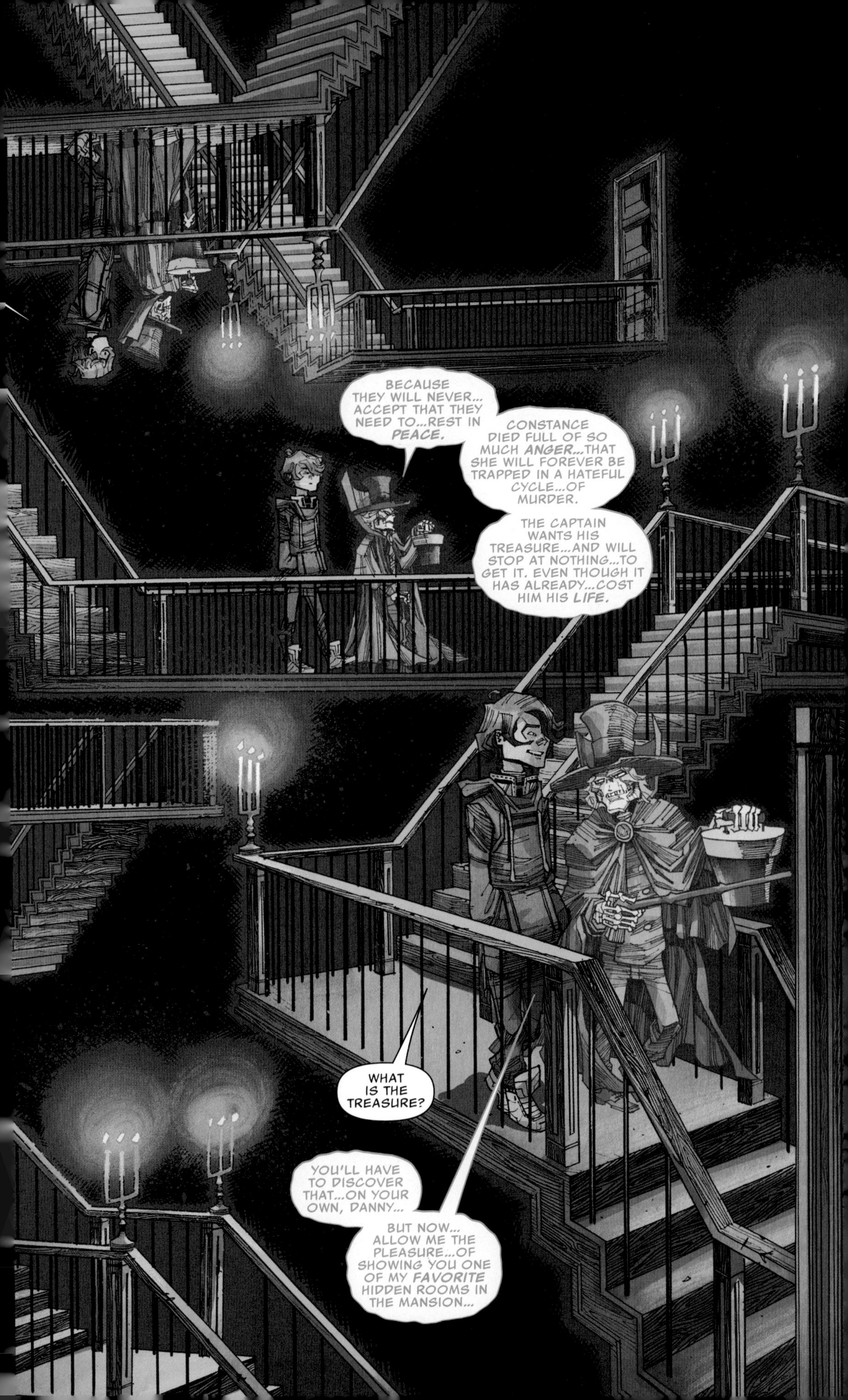
BECAUSE THEY WILL NEVER... ACCEPT THAT THEY NEED TO...REST IN PEACE.
CONSTANCE DIED FULL OF SO MUCH ANGER...THAT SHE WILL FOREVER BE TRAPPED IN A HATEFUL CYCLE...OF MURDER.
THE CAPTAIN WANTS HIS TREASURE...AND WILL STOP AT NOTHING...TO GET IT. EVEN THOUGH IT HAS ALREADY...COST HIM HIS LIFE.
WHAT IS THE TREASURE?
YOU'LL HAVE TO DISCOVER THAT...ON YOUR OWN, DANNY...
BUT NOW... ALLOW ME THE PLEASURE...OF SHOWING YOU ONE OF MY FAVORITE HIDDEN ROOMS IN THE MANSION...

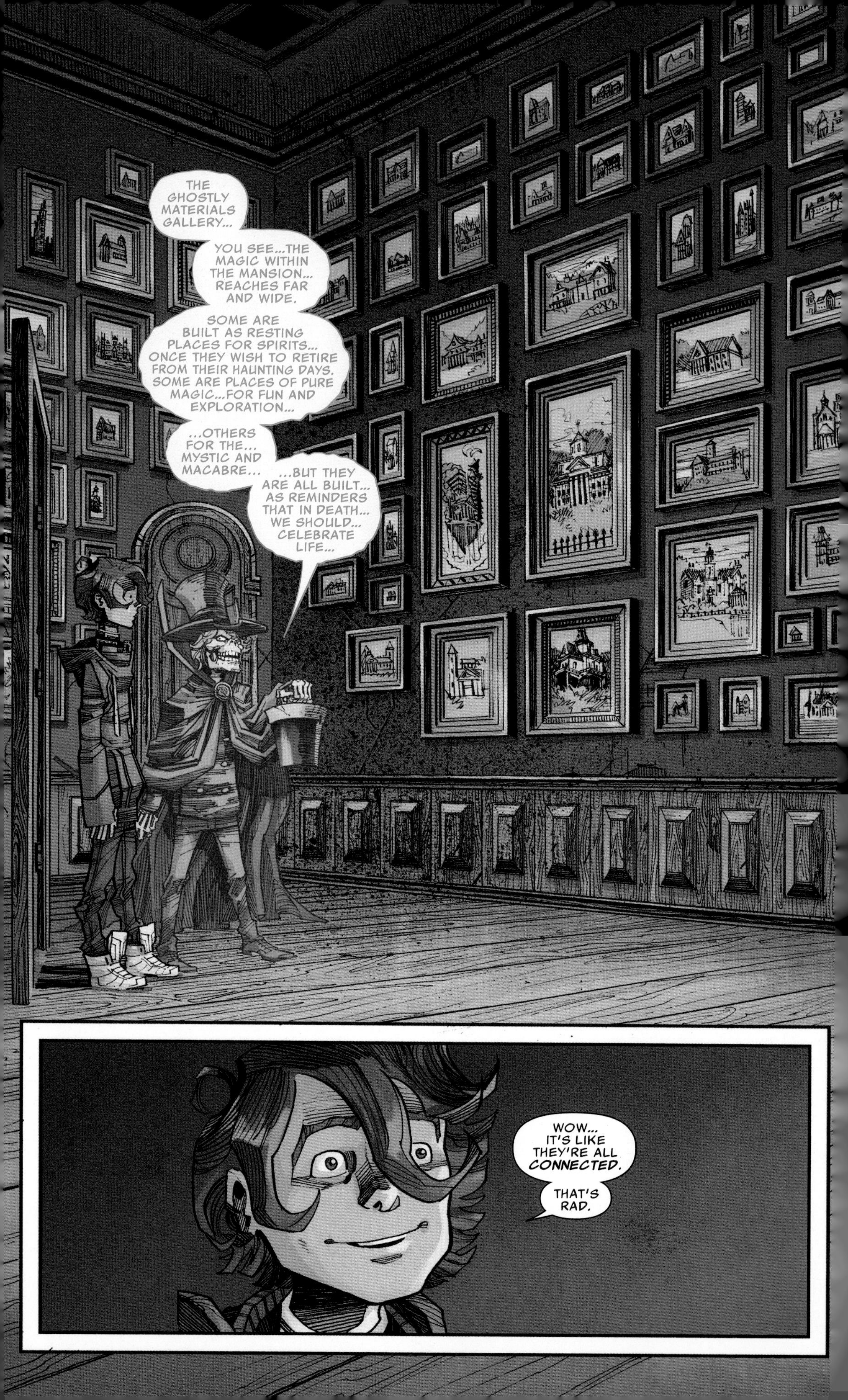
THE GHOSTLY MATERIALS GALLERY...
YOU SEE...THE MAGIC WITHIN THE MANSION... REACHES FAR AND WIDE.
SOME ARE BUILT AS RESTING PLACES FOR SPIRITS... ONCE THEY WISH TO RETIRE FROM THEIR HAUNTING DAYS. SOME ARE PLACES OF PURE MAGIC...FOR FUN AND EXPLORATION...
...OTHERS FOR THE... MYSTIC AND MACABRE...
...BUT THEY ARE ALL BUILT... AS REMINDERS THAT IN DEATH... WE SHOULD... CELEBRATE LIFE...
WOW... IT'S LIKE THEY'RE ALL CONNECTED.
THAT'S RAD.

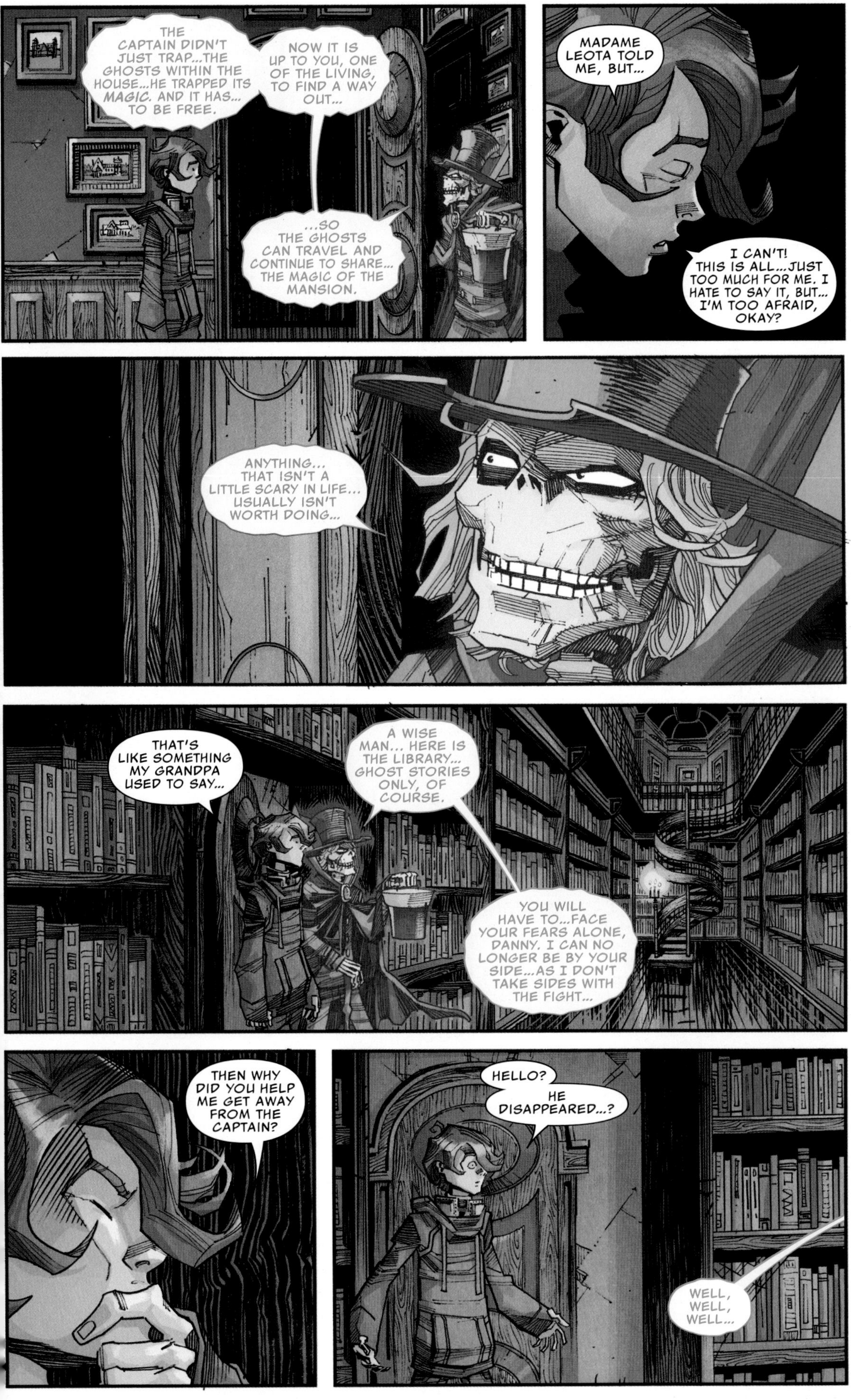
THE CAPTAIN DIDN'T JUST TRAP...THE GHOSTS WITHIN THE HOUSE...HE TRAPPED ITS MAGIC. AND IT HAS... TO BE FREE.
NOW IT IS UP TO YOU, ONE OF THE LIVING, TO FIND A WAY OUT...
...SO THE GHOSTS CAN TRAVEL AND CONTINUE TO SHARE... THE MAGIC OF THE MANSION.
MADAME LEOTA TOLD ME, BUT...
I CAN'T! THIS IS ALL...JUST TOO MUCH FOR ME. I HATE TO SAY IT, BUT... I'M TOO AFRAID, OKAY?
ANYTHING... THAT ISN'T A LITTLE SCARY IN LIFE... USUALLY ISN'T WORTH DOING...
THAT'S LIKE SOMETHING MY GRANDPA USED TO SAY...
A WISE MAN... HERE IS THE LIBRARY... GHOST STORIES ONLY, OF COURSE.
YOU WILL HAVE TO...FACE YOUR FEARS ALONE, DANNY. I CAN NO LONGER BE BY YOUR SIDE...AS I DON'T TAKE SIDES WITH THE FIGHT...
THEN WHY DID YOU HELP ME GET AWAY FROM THE CAPTAIN?
HELLO?
HE DISAPPEARED...?
WELL, WELL, WELL...

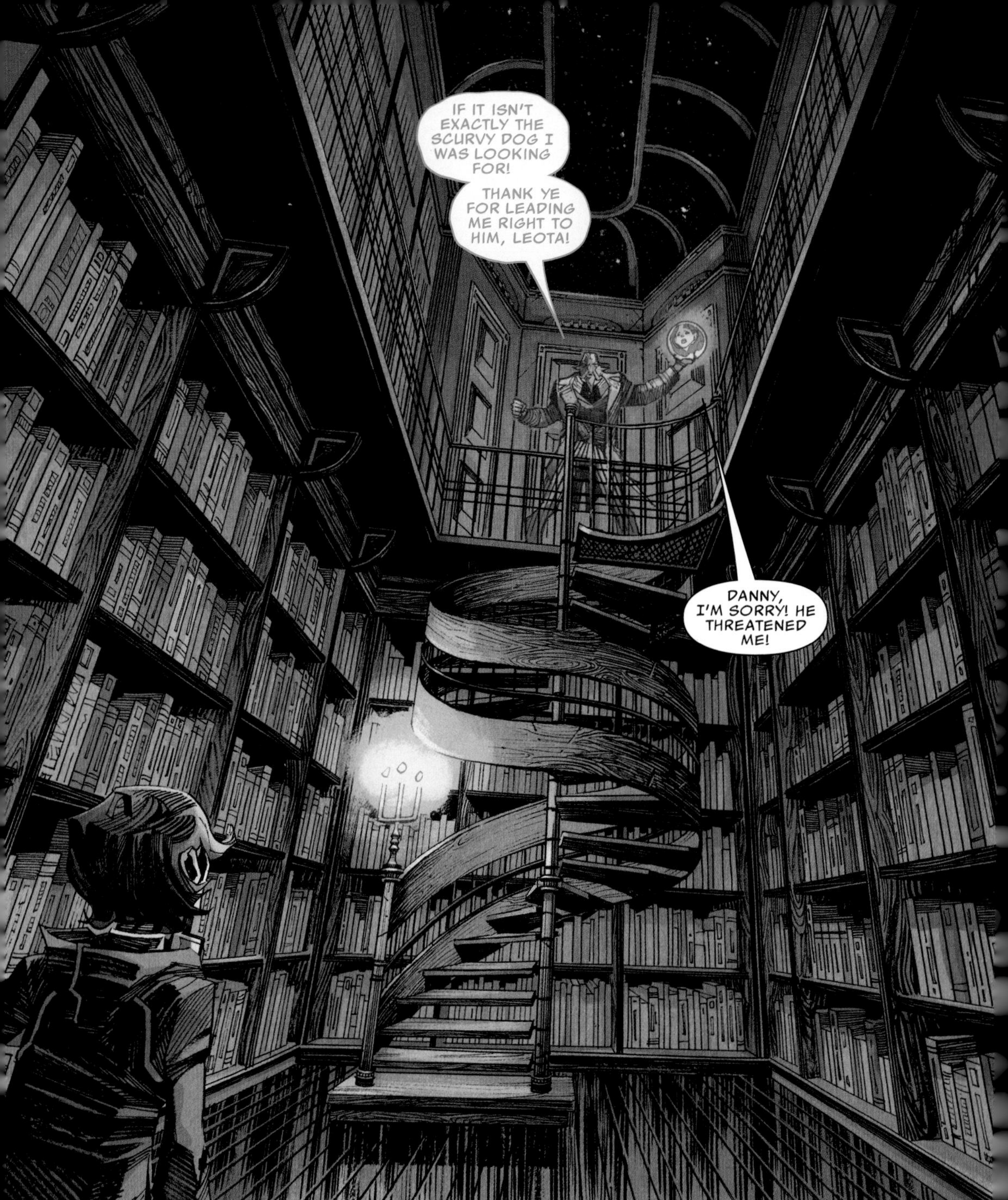
IF IT ISN'T EXACTLY THE SCURVY DOG I WAS LOOKING FOR!
THANK YE FOR LEADING ME RIGHT TO HIM, LEOTA!
DANNY, I'M SORRY! HE THREATENED ME!

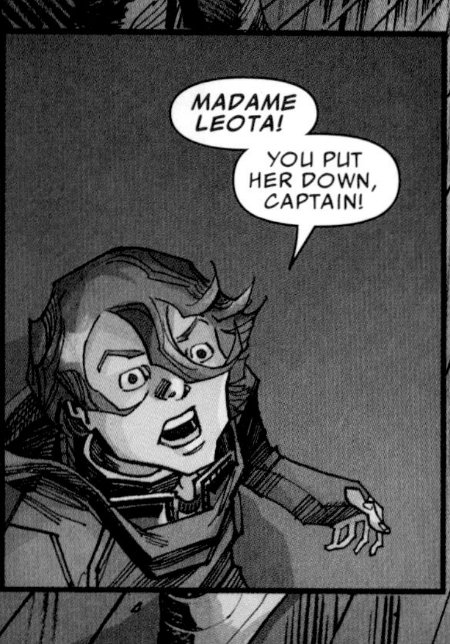
MADAME LEOTA!
YOU PUT HER DOWN, CAPTAIN!

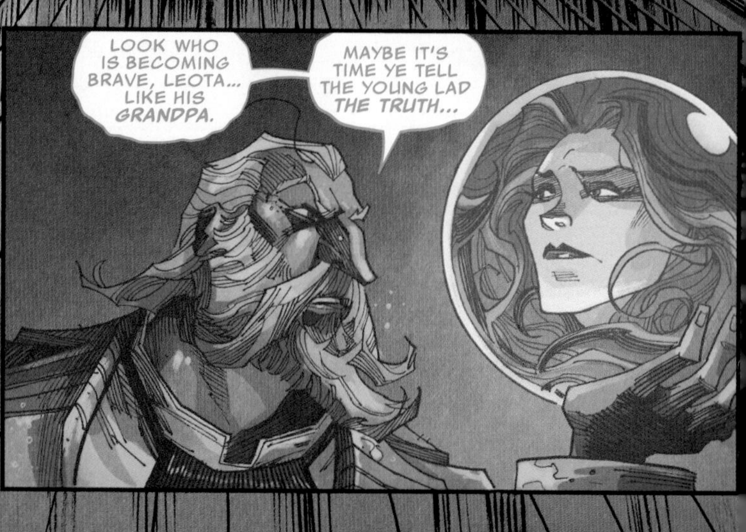
LOOK WHO IS BECOMING BRAVE, LEOTA... LIKE HIS GRANDPA.
MAYBE IT'S TIME YE TELL THE YOUNG LAD THE TRUTH...

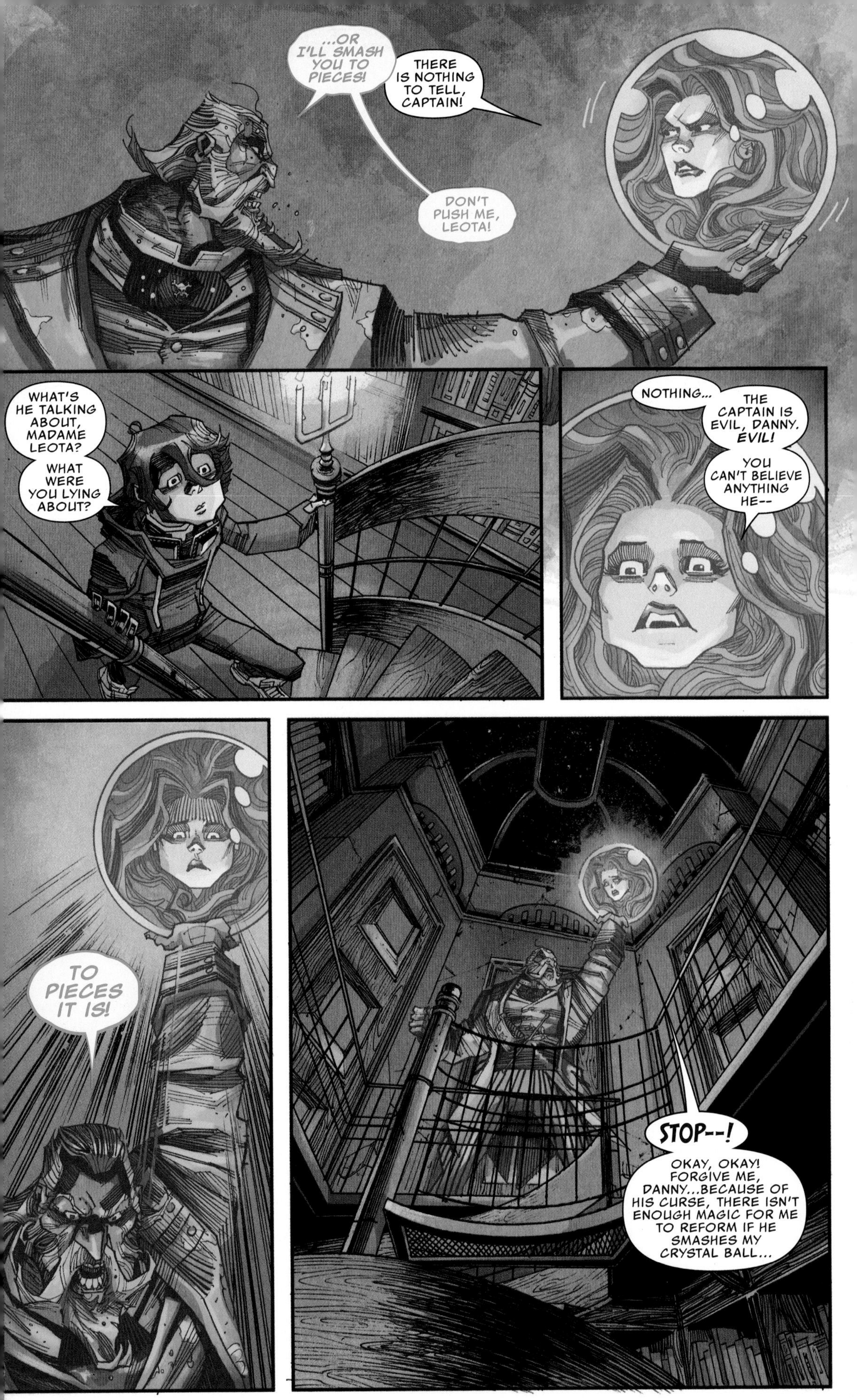
...OR I'LL SMASH YOU TO PIECES!
THERE IS NOTHING TO TELL, CAPTAIN!
DON'T PUSH ME, LEOTA!
WHAT'S HE TALKING ABOUT, MADAME LEOTA?
WHAT WERE YOU LYING ABOUT?
NOTHING...
THE CAPTAIN IS EVIL, DANNY. EVIL!
YOU CAN'T BELIEVE ANYTHING HE--
TO PIECES IT IS!
STOP--!
OKAY, OKAY! FORGIVE ME, DANNY...BECAUSE OF HIS CURSE, THERE ISN'T ENOUGH MAGIC FOR ME TO REFORM IF HE SMASHES MY CRYSTAL BALL...

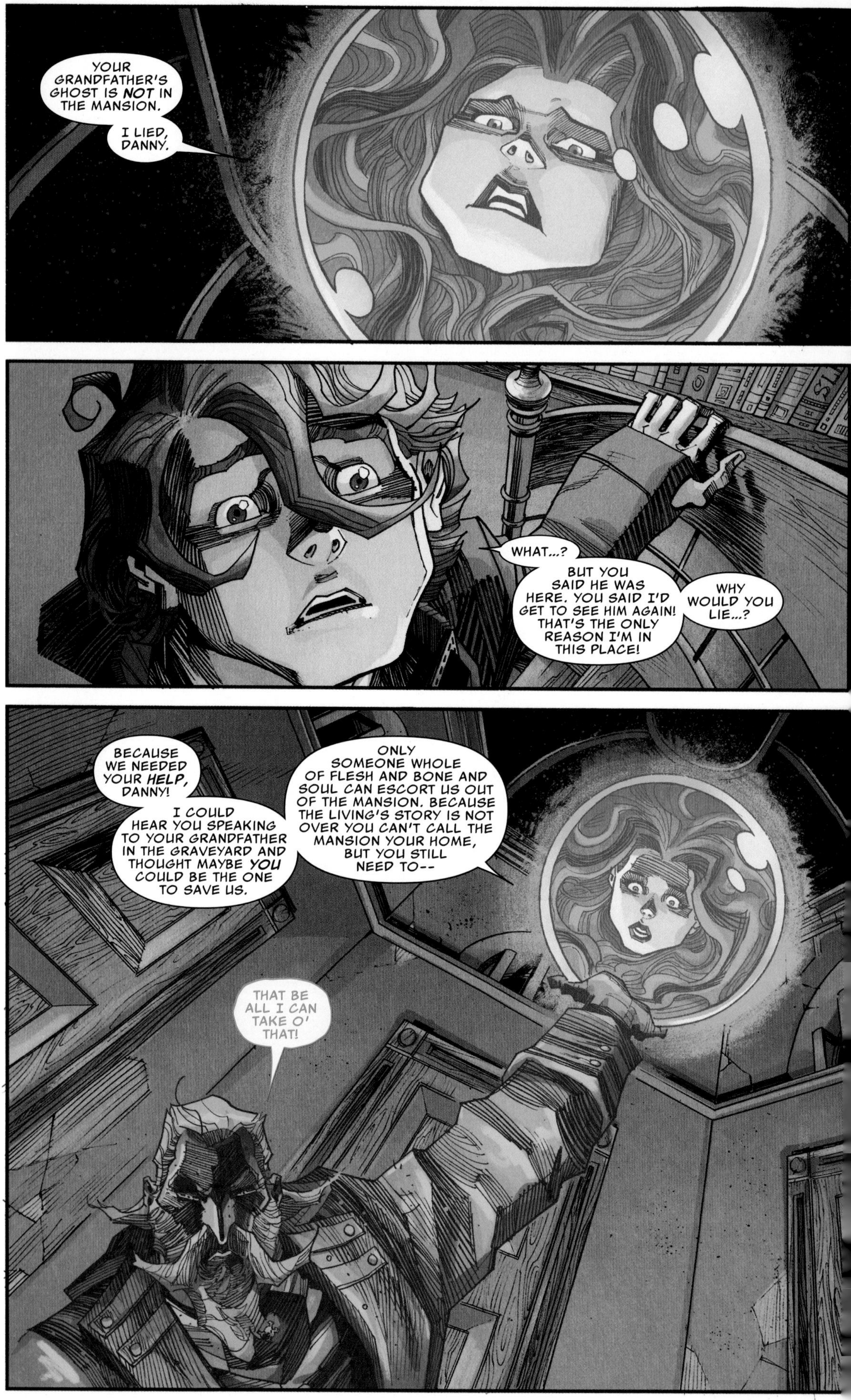
YOUR GRANDFATHER'S GHOST IS *NOT* IN THE MANSION.
I LIED, DANNY.
WHAT...?
BUT YOU SAID HE WAS HERE. YOU SAID I'D GET TO SEE HIM AGAIN! THAT'S THE ONLY REASON I'M IN THIS PLACE!
WHY WOULD YOU LIE...?
BECAUSE WE NEEDED YOUR *HELP*, DANNY!
I COULD HEAR YOU SPEAKING TO YOUR GRANDFATHER IN THE GRAVEYARD AND THOUGHT MAYBE *YOU* COULD BE THE ONE TO SAVE US.
ONLY SOMEONE WHOLE OF FLESH AND BONE AND SOUL CAN ESCORT US OUT OF THE MANSION. BECAUSE THE LIVING'S STORY IS NOT OVER YOU CAN'T CALL THE MANSION YOUR HOME, BUT YOU STILL NEED TO--
THAT BE ALL I CAN TAKE O' THAT!

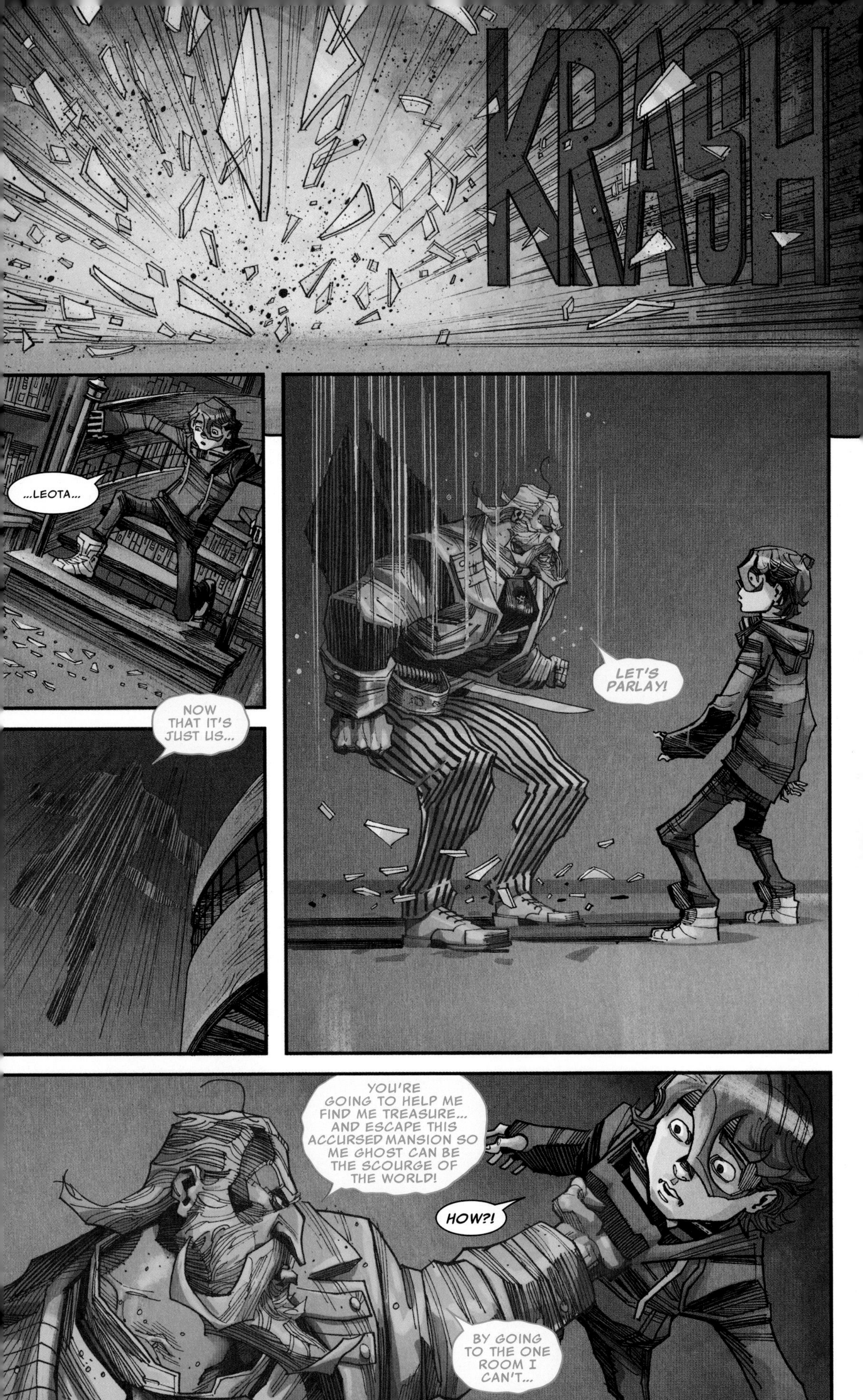
KRASH
...LEOTA...
NOW THAT IT'S JUST US...
LET'S PARLAY!
YOU'RE GOING TO HELP ME FIND ME TREASURE... AND ESCAPE THIS ACCURSED MANSION SO ME GHOST CAN BE THE SCOURGE OF THE WORLD!
HOW?!
BY GOING TO THE ONE ROOM I CAN'T...

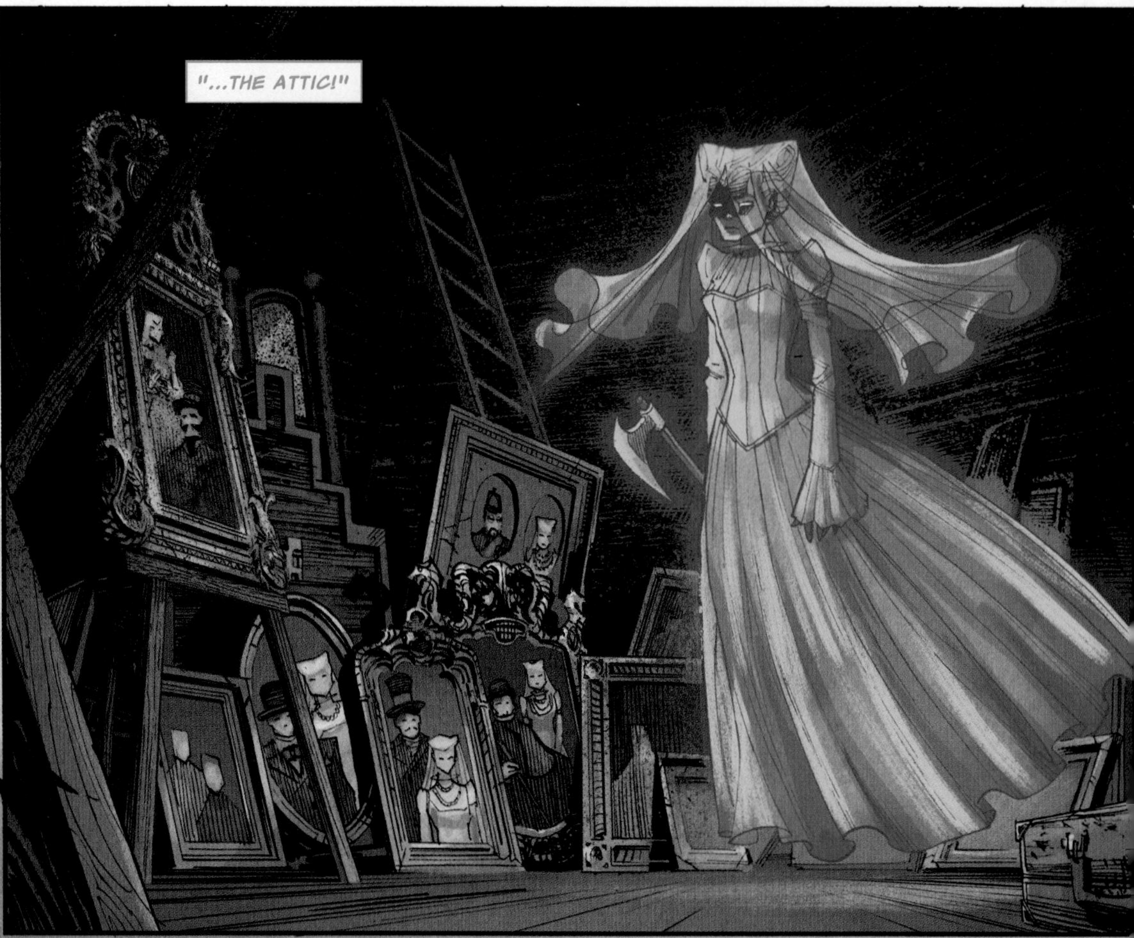
"...THE ATTIC!"

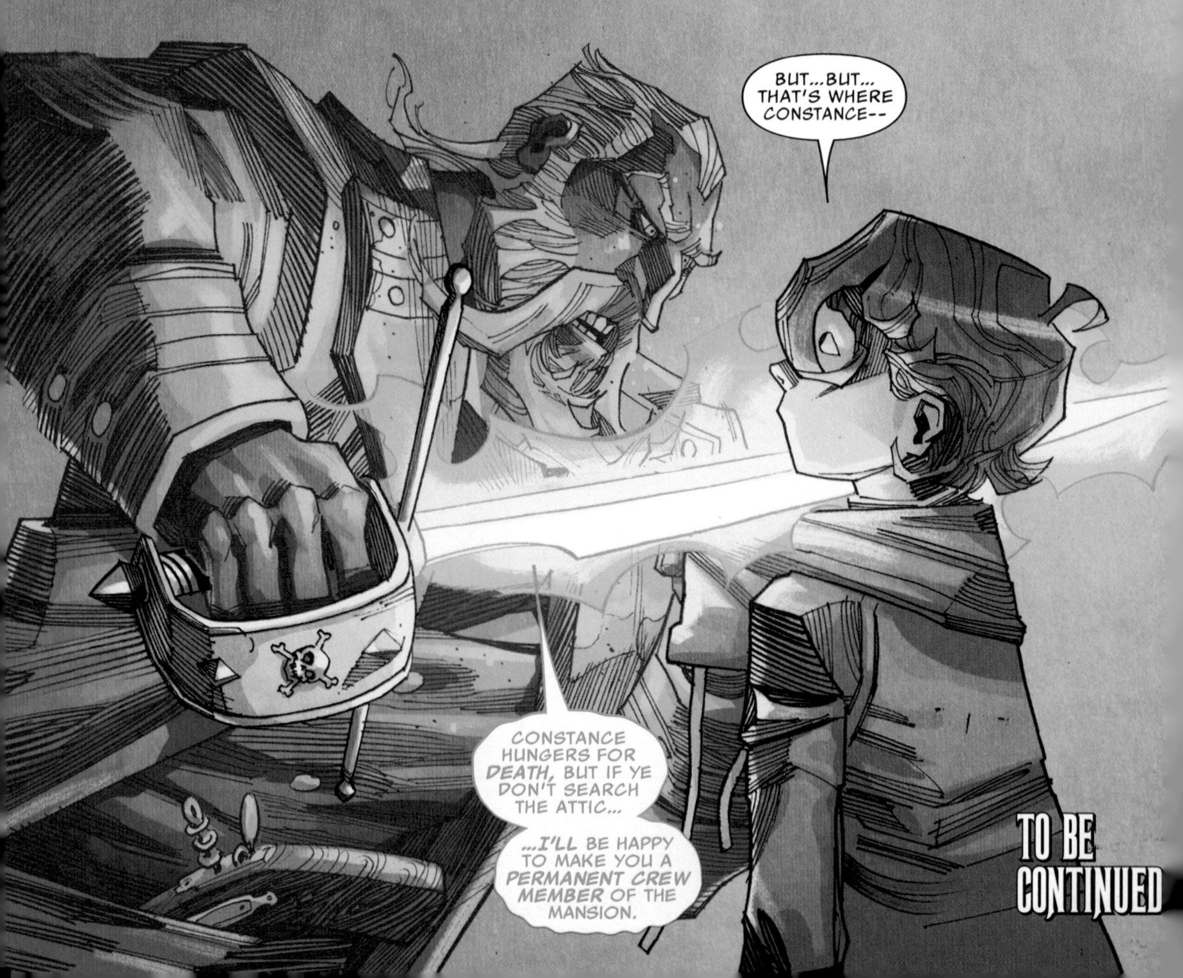
BUT...BUT... THAT'S WHERE CONSTANCE--
CONSTANCE HUNGERS FOR DEATH, BUT IF YE DON'T SEARCH THE ATTIC...
...I'LL BE HAPPY TO MAKE YOU A PERMANENT CREW MEMBER OF THE MANSION.
TO BE CONTINUED

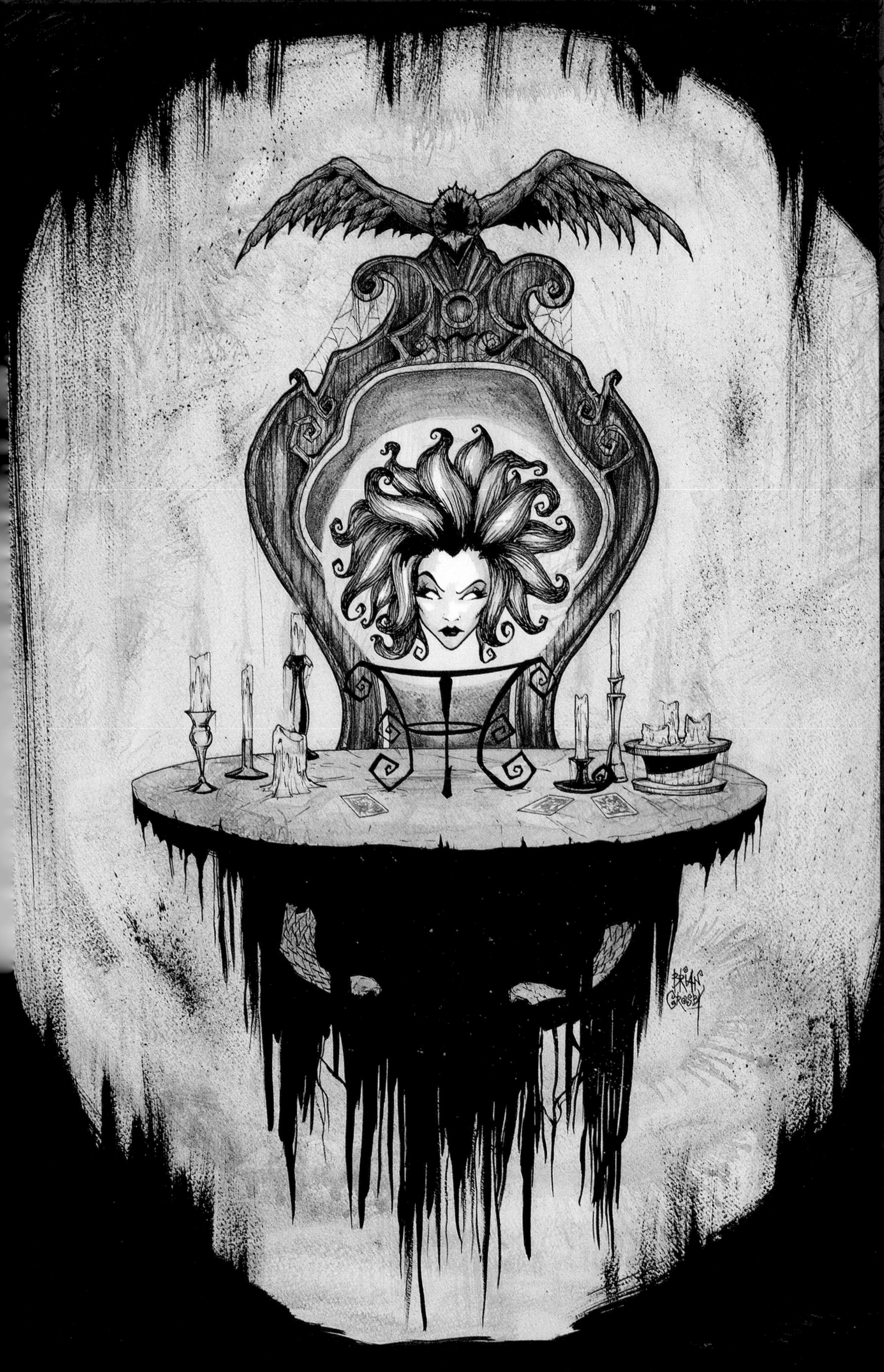
BRIAN CROSBY

No. 3 Variant by
Brian Crosby.

The Haunted Mansion

COLLECT THEM ALL!

Set of 5 Hardcover Books ISBN: 978-1-61479-586-5

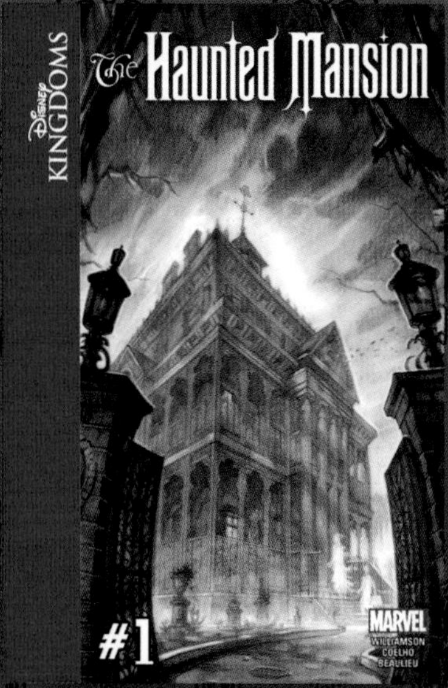
The Haunted Mansion
Disney KINGDOMS
#1
MARVEL
WILLIAMSON
COELHO
BEAULIEU

Hardcover Book ISBN
978-1-61479-587-2

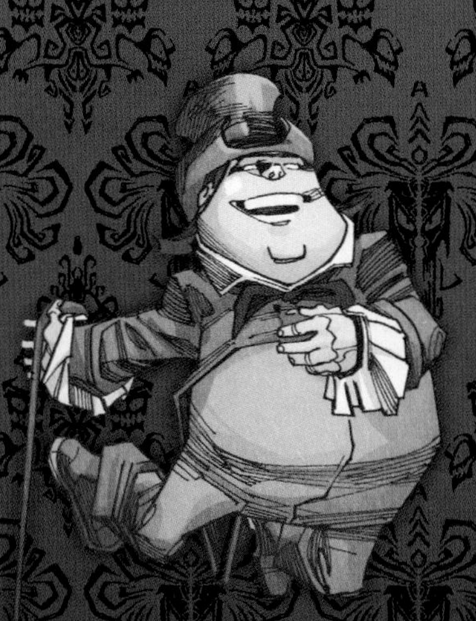

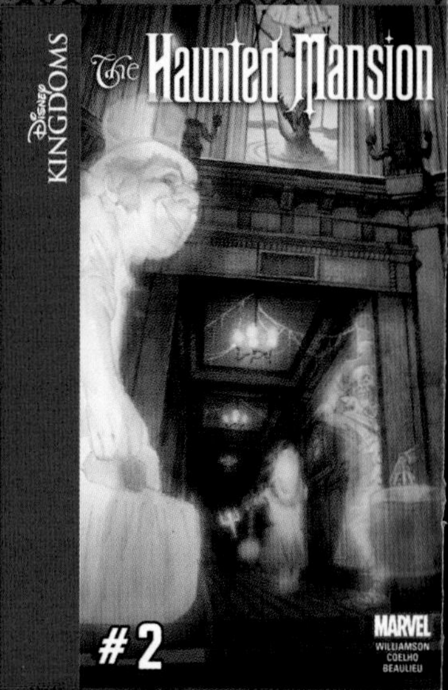
The Haunted Mansion
Disney KINGDOMS
#2
MARVEL
WILLIAMSON
COELHO
BEAULIEU

Hardcover Book ISBN
978-1-61479-588-9

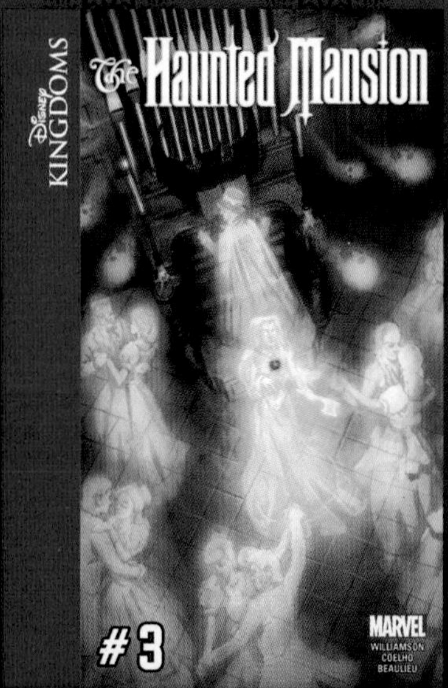
The Haunted Mansion
Disney KINGDOMS
#3
MARVEL
WILLIAMSON
COELHO
BEAULIEU

Hardcover Book ISBN
978-1-61479-589-6

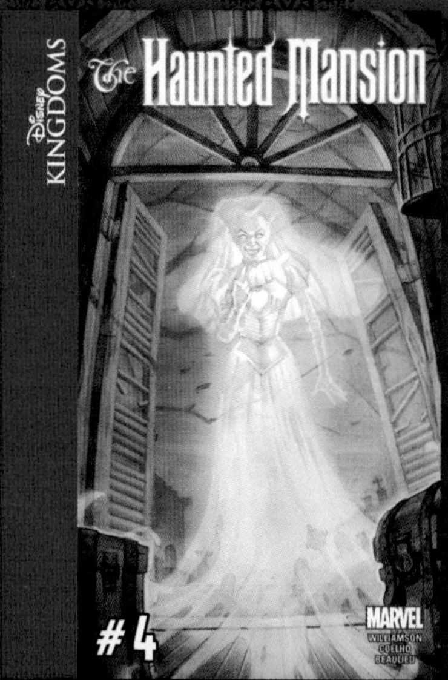
The Haunted Mansion
Disney KINGDOMS
#4
MARVEL
WILLIAMSON
COELHO
BEAULIEU

Hardcover Book ISBN
978-1-61479-590-2

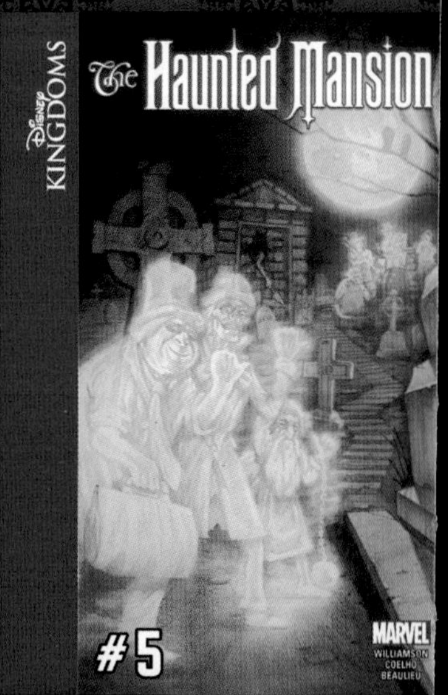
The Haunted Mansion
Disney KINGDOMS
#5
MARVEL
WILLIAMSON
COELHO
BEAULIEU

Hardcover Book ISBN
978-1-61479-591-9